Rabén & Sjögren Stockholm

Translation copyright © 1994 by Joan Sandin
All rights reserved
Originally published in Sweden by Rabén & Sjögren
under the title *Store-Nalles Bok,* copyright © 1988 by Christina Björk
Printed in Hungary
Library of Congress catalog card number: 94-66897
First edition, 1994

ISBN 91 29 62912 8

CHRISTINA BJÖRK

Big Bear's Book

BY HIMSELF

Afterword by Johan Cullberg
Translated by Joan Sandin

R&S
BOOKS

Stockholm   New York   London   Adelaide   Toronto

For us, to whom our childhood
has meant so much,
the journey back is short,
the coming and going easy.

Christopher Milne in *The Enchanted Places*

Contents

Foreword

My friend Christina and I have argued back and forth about which of us should tell this story.

Now I've decided it has to be me.

Otherwise, there will never be a teddy-bear book. Christina has been trying to write one for more than ten years. That's how it is, she says, with those things that are closest to your heart; you always write about something else, instead.

So if there's ever going to be a book, I'm going to have to be the one to start it. Then we'll see what happens. If there's anything I don't know enough about (whatever *that* might be), Christina says she can always take over.

The sad thing about this book is that Christina's father is no longer living. He died in 1980. I know he would have liked to read about us

Christina's father

teddy bears (and about himself). He's going to be appearing in this book a lot, since he knew us so well. He gave many of us to Christina.

Christina's father always kept track of all our names (including our Latin names), and who was married to whom, and who was related to whom. That's because he was interested in genealogy (the study of family ties). He had traced Christina's ancestors all the way back to Aunt Lejonstolpe (we laughed a lot about the name; it means *lionpole*), and Barbro Stigsdotter. (She was the woman who helped Gustavus Vasa to escape by hoisting him down through the outhouse in Ornässtugan. Gustavus Vasa, who was leading a struggle for Swedish independence from Denmark, later became King of Sweden.)

It was also Christina's father who made up all the teddy-bear stories, so actually he could have been the one to write this book. But he had this idea that he had to go to the office every day, so he never had the time.

Now Christina's father is gone, but we still think about him a lot. That's why we've decided (I think it was Little Bear's idea) that this book should be dedicated to him. After all, it was mostly because of him that we teddy bears were so very important at home. Maybe it's even because of him that Christina and I started writing.

Thanks, Christina's father!

Stockholm, February 1988

Big Bear

> In Memory of
> Christina's
> Father
>
> Who was also called
> Hans Lundberg

How Christina Got Us

Now, don't think you're going to find out how Christina got us in this chapter (I just thought the first chapter ought to be called that). It's all very mysterious. We teddy bears don't really remember, and Christina has no idea.

"You've just always been here," says Christina.

And we can't ask Christina's father either, even though we know that he gave some of us to her. We're just not sure which ones. We tried to ask Christina's mother, but she's lost almost all her memory. She only remembers things from her *own* childhood. (For example, that her doll was named Goldie, and that she got her from Aunt Dea.) She can't remember how Christina got us. It's funny how people lose their memories: they first forget the most recent things that happen; the oldest memories stay.

"Wait a minute," says Christina. "I just remembered when I got Teddy Yellow. But by then I already had you. And Little Bear and Huggy Yellow, Little Yellow and Baby Yellow and Snow White and Baby Snow White.

"But I've heard," Christina continues, "that Baby Snow White was my very first teddy bear; I got him when I was just a little baby. I loved to lie and chew on his long skinny feet. But when did I ever get the rest of you?"

Well, you should always find out about important things before people die or lose their memories.

In any case, I think we arrived pretty early, when Christina still lived on New Street in Södertälje. She was only two or three years old then. Later we all moved to Pipers Street in Stockholm.

"There is, however, *proof* in my case," says Huggy Yellow. "There are pictures of me — two of them, with

*Christina
and
Huggy Yellow
1940*

Christina. In one we're sitting in a stroller, and in the other one Christina's about to lose her pants. But she's holding me tight in both pictures. It's just too bad I'm a little out of focus," says Huggy Yellow.

But now I think I'd better introduce us the right way, one at a time. (Maybe someone out there thinks we have silly names, but it was actually Christina who made them up.) Well then, I'll start by introducing myself.

Helarctos malayanus

Big Bear (Me)

I am one of those (for teddy bears) unusual breeds called the sun bear (*Helarctos malayanus*). Identifying characteristics are our long pointed noses, which are much lighter in color than the rest of our coats. We are also somewhat slimmer than the brown bear (*Ursus arctos*).

Ursus arctos

I was named Big Bear because of my size. I was the biggest of all of Christina's teddy bears. And probably the smartest as well. I recall that I was the most thoughtful and responsible one. I was a sort of head of the teddy-bear bureau (and the little-red-doll bureau), a kind of teddy-bear bureau chief. I was the kind of boss that Christina's father was at his job.

With time, I became pretty skinny. My excelsior stuffing got all crushed and my body, arms, and legs became sort of limp. Now and then, Christina's mother said I should be cut open and restuffed with new excelsior, so I'd be able to sit up a little better. But Christina wouldn't hear of it, no. She thought I was just fine the way I was.

If they'd asked me, I'd have said I would love some new soles; my old ones are all worn out.

Huggy Yellow

In the beginning her name was Huggy Boy, and she was a he. She's a typical *huggy bear,* which I don't think has a Latin name, and is found only among teddy bears.

But then Christina got Teddy Yellow, and he needed a wife. Huggy Boy became Huggy Yellow. Maybe she had been a girl all along, but we just hadn't noticed.

Huggy Yellow had bad eyes. When they fell off, Christina's mother sewed on new ones. She used some buttons from an old moth-eaten sweater. Those buttons looked a lot like red eyes with black eyelashes, so now Huggy Yellow really did look like a little lady with her new eyes and a flower over her ear. (The sweater that she's wearing was knitted later by Christina.)

Teddy Yellow

It was Christmas Eve when Teddy Yellow arrived. That was fun! I remember exactly: it was the Christmas Christina also got a kaleidoscope, and a little linen cabinet for our sheets and towels.

On Christmas morning we all lay in Christina's bed, looking through the kaleidoscope and getting acquainted with Teddy Yellow. Nobody knows if it was Christina's mother or father who bought him, but we're sure he came from Oskarson's Department Store. Christina had smart parents: they understood that, even though she already had seven teddy bears, she needed one more.

Teddy Yellow was a *very decent* teddy bear, even if he was a newcomer. Maybe he wasn't so well educated (had never heard of Latin or Teddy-Bear Tales), but he and Huggy Yellow made a perfect couple.

Little Yellow

As soon as Teddy Yellow came, you could see that Little Yellow had to be his and Huggy Yellow's son. Little Yellow was a nice but rather boring little boy. He couldn't turn his head: he always looked straight ahead. That was because his head and body were made all in one piece. In the beginning he could move his arms and legs, but then they fell off. Christina's mother had to sew them back on, and after that, they were a lot harder to turn.

Little Yellow had inherited Huggy Yellow's bad eyes. But Christina's father fixed that by painting new eyes on him with black ink. Christina thought that was awful, but at least poor Little Yellow could see again.

Baby Yellow

Suddenly Huggy Girl and Teddy Yellow had another baby. He was born at Tivoli Amusement Park when Christina pulled on a string in one of the booths and got Baby Yellow for her prize. He was so little, and he was holding a baby bottle in his paws. His body was made of plaster covered with fur. He couldn't get wet, poor little thing.

Baby Yellow got into a lot more trouble than his big brother. He was always getting lost because he was so little and mischievous. The first thing he did was lose his bottle.

Once he was lost for several years. When he returned, he had grown and looked like the smallest-size Steiff bear (the kind that have a little metal button in the left ear, though Baby Yellow had lost his, of course). When Christina learned to sew, she made him a pair of red-and-white overalls.

*Here is the whole family, with
Baby Yellow probably taking off
for somewhere else again.
One time (much later, when
Christina was grown up), he disappeared just as she was about to
tape a television program for
children about teddy bears. So
Huggy Yellow had to sit there in
the studio and report with a
shaking voice:
"We did have another son — a
little one with red-and-white-
checked overalls. But he's lost.
It's all so terrible …
If you should see a little huggy —
sniff — teddy bear in red-and-
white-checked overalls — sniff —
then it* must *be Baby Yellow —
sniff — and if so, please let us
know!"
Christina searched for several
days. The exact same day the program was to be on TV, she found
Baby Yellow hidden in an old
cigar box. She rushed over to the
TV station and gave Baby Yellow
to the announcer.
At the end of the show, the
announcer held up Baby Yellow
and said:
"I have some late-breaking and
wonderful news:
Baby Yellow has been found!
You can imagine how happy his
family is. And that's our program
for today."
Well, it certainly was lucky that
he was found.
That show would have been much
too sad otherwise.
At least, Christina would never
have been able to watch it when
she was a child …
(And I don't dare tell you what
happened when it was shown as a
rerun.)*

14

Snow White

Thalarctos maritimus

ow we've come to the White family. They're polar bears, *Thalarctos maritimus.* Snow White is a rare teddy bear, because she walks on all fours. She has a brown spot on one side. Here's how she got it:

One day Christina was pretending that all the teddy bears were jumping over a pit, from sofa to bed. Her father played for a while, too, but I remember he got tired of the game and left.

We bears and Christina continued jumping higher and higher. Suddenly Snow White jumped all the way up to the ceiling and landed on the lampshade. Then Christina decided that we all should jump up there. I think that took several hours.

Then Christina collapsed on the bed, all tired out. That was when her father came in again.

"Where are all the teddy bears?" he asked.

"There," said Christina, pointing up at the light.

"They can't stay there," said her father. "They'll burn themselves on the light bulb."

"Oh!" said Christina. "Take them down fast!"

When we got down, we saw that poor Snow White had a brown spot on her side, because she had been lying closest to the light bulb.

Baby Snow White and Snow White

Baby Snow White

aby Snow White is, of course, Snow White's son. Sometimes Christina felt sorry for Baby Snow White because he didn't have a father. So she would decide that I should be his father and be married to Snow White. But we never fit together all that well, Snow White and I.

"How can a brown bear like me have a white son?"

"He's an *albino,* of course," said Christina.

16

She said that because her father had told her that animals (and people, too) can sometimes be born without any pigment (skin and eye color). A brown elk, for example, can have an all-white calf.

"But Baby Snow White doesn't even have red eyes," I said. "Albinos usually have red eyes."

So Christina came up with the idea that I had adopted Baby Snow White.

That's the way it was until she read *Winnie-the-Pooh*. Then she started pretending that she was Christopher Robin and Baby Snow White was Pooh.

"Hey, I adopted him, remember?" I said.

"That was *then*," said Christina. "Now he goes under the name of Sanders. Your name isn't Sanders, is it?"

"No."

"Well then," said Christina.

"I think he's more like Piglet," I said.

"Don't be stupid," said Christina.

Piglet in Winnie-the-Pooh

Even though he is so small, Baby Snow White has lived a long life and seen a lot. He started by getting his toes bitten by Christina.

When Christina was just a year old, her mother got really ill and was in the hospital for a long time. None of us can remember what happened to Christina and to all of us teddy bears then. For part of the time we definitely stayed with Aunt Ki.

It was there that Baby Snow White accidentally fell behind a radiator. When Christina's mother was a little better, we got to go home, and Nurse Julia took care of Christina and us teddy bears. (Except for Baby Snow White, who was still behind the radiator at Aunt Ki's house.)

When Christina was four years old, she lived with Aunt Ki again for a while. One day she stuck Uncle Sune's cane in behind the radiator and something wonderful happened: Baby Snow White popped up.

"Christina!" he squealed. "You finally found me!"

Little Bear and Jacob

I don't know the Latin name for Little Bear's breed either. *Nobody* knows how he looked in the beginning, if he was yellow or brown or white. He slept in Christina's bed and he got to be a real mess. He lost his eyes and ears, and his nose got all squashed. All his fur disappeared.

Then Grandma took care of him, re-covering him with an old tricot undershirt. It wasn't long before he was worn out again. This time she re-covered him in a flowered material. After that, he was marbled like her chairs, then purple like her easy chair. Then Christina's mother took over and made Little Bear a suit out of silver lamé (from her evening gown). That was *not* a good idea; Little Bear was shiny and felt like a cold fish in bed. And when the silver tarnished, he turned sort of green.

Then Christina's mother used one of the catskins Christina's father put on his back when he had a backache. Since then, Little Bear has been covered with catskin. We think he looks nice, but other people think he looks strange.

When Christina grew up and married, her husband told her: "Now you have to decide which one of us you want in bed — me or Filthy Bear."

And imagine, she chose the husband. That was the start of sad times for us teddy bears. (I'll get back to that.)

Little Bear's best friend was named Jacob. He was a monkey hand puppet. Christina's father had a Jacob just like him when he was little.

Little Bear and Jacob slept in Christina's bed every night at that time. But they were often out having adventures on their flying carpet. (I'll get back to that as well.)

Close-up of Little Bear's paw

Uncle Harry's Teddy Bear

I have to warn all sensitive readers that this is a sad chapter.

When Christina was little, she got a green plush teddy bear from Uncle Harry. Uncle Harry was Christina's dad's boyhood friend. They had played in the sandbox together. (It's impossible to imagine those two gentlemen playing in a sandbox!) They were in the same class in school. (There's a picture of them to prove it.) When they grew up, Uncle Harry became a music director, and Christina's dad became a bureau director. Uncle Harry played the organ at his job, which Christina's dad definitely *didn't* do (but I don't know what Christina's dad actually did at his job).

Uncle Harry's Teddy Bear

I notice that I start talking about other things when I should be writing about Uncle Harry's Teddy Bear. It's not an easy thing to talk about.

As I was saying, green plush. His mouth was always open, so it looked as if he was laughing all the time. And he had checked overalls. Christina and all of us teddy bears liked him a lot; he was such an unusually happy bear.

After a while, Uncle Harry's Teddy Bear got a little hole in his shoulder. Nobody thought much about it. Until sawdust started running out of the hole.

One day Uncle Harry's Teddy Bear was gone. Christina searched for days. When she asked her parents if they had seen him, they didn't really answer. "He's probably lost," they said.

"Lost," said Christina. "He can't possibly be lost. He never even goes out. He must be here at home somewhere."

"No, he's probably lost," said her father.

"It doesn't really matter," said her mother. "He was all worn out, anyway."

"Yes, he was so messy," said her father.

Then Christina understood.

"You took him!" she screamed. "You took him! You took him!"

Christina's dad (1) and Uncle Harry (2) in second grade, 1917

Christina carried on like that, screaming and crying, for several hours. We teddy bears were also very upset. So were Christina's parents. They probably began to understand that they had done something dumb.

For a long time after that happened, Christina was very worried about us teddy bears. As soon as we got a little rip, we would have to hide. Christina was very careful not to let her parents see.

Eventually she got over it, and that was lucky, because we really did need to be repaired now and then. Arms had to be sewn on tighter. Soles needed to be fixed, ears and eyes checked. Not to mention all the re-coverings Little Bear had to go through.

Nothing that sad ever happened again in our family.

 One day, not too long ago, Christina came home and told us that she had seen an exhibit at the toy museum. And there she had seen a teddy bear that looked *exactly* like Uncle Harry's Teddy Bear.

"Maybe it *was* him," said Huggy Yellow.

"No," said Christina. "His clothes were different."

"Maybe he changed his clothes," I said.

"No, he could never do that," said Christina. "They were sewn on. But I'm almost sure it was Uncle Harry's Teddy Bear's brother."

Christina's Flying Rug

Every night there was always the same routine in Christina's bedroom.

"Remember that this is a *bedroom*," Christina told us as she got undressed, "and not a *bedwoom,* like little kids say."

Then Christina crawled into bed with Little Bear and Jacob. The rest of us sat around in our little doll chairs. Sometimes the little bears slept in the dollhouse.

Then Christina's dad would come in and tell a story. Usually Christina wanted a Little Bear and Jacob story. Those stories always begin and end exactly the same way, but in between anything at all can happen.

It always starts with Christina falling asleep and Little Bear and Jacob climbing out of bed down to the rug.

Jacob and Little Bear in bed

Little Bear and Jacob Fly South

(A Little Bear and Jacob Story)

Before Jacob had even made himself comfortable on the rug, Little Bear started saying the verse:

"Abracadabra, misinka misoo, sibbeday sibbido,
extra lara, Kathy Klara, rug bug pabulum-ugh,
out with you, my long long MAN!"

And just as he said MAN, the rug would lift up and fly out the bedroom window. It flew over the city and out to the suburbs, and then even farther. Soon they could see big fields and small farms below them.

"Wonder where we'll end up tonight," said Little Bear. "It can't be

Norrland, because I don't see any forests."

"And it can't be Yaughtland, because there aren't any boats," said Jacob.

"There's no such place as Yaughtland," said Little Bear. "You must mean Gotland."

"No way. I didn't mean that at all," said Jacob. "I meant Scotland. Look how everything is plaid down there."

"The *country* isn't plaid," said Little Bear. "It's only the *kilts* that are plaid. No, I think we are over some farms in southern Sweden."

"Doesn't matter," said Jacob, "because up ahead there's a giant house that we're about to run into …"

"*Abracadabra!*" cried Little Bear, hoping it would keep them from crashing into the huge gray stone castle.

"*Hick Vick palublum-ick,*" Jacob added helpfully, but as usual it was all wrong. Instead of lifting up, the rug tipped over as it was flying above the chimney, and the fringe got stuck on an old wagon wheel and a lot of branches that were on top of the chimney.

"If storks weren't so rare, I would say this was a stork's nest," said Little Bear.

"If it weren't for that stick-like thing flying over there, I wouldn't think so either," said Jacob.

A large stork landed in the nest. It snapped Jacob up in its beak and started throwing him up in the air. At least *seven* times the stork tossed Jacob up in the air.

"Stop!" screamed Little Bear, hitting the stork on the leg. "Be careful of Jacob. He's a fragile old monkey."

"Sorry," said the stork. "I thought he was a frog."

The rug approaches Glimminge Castle

And with that he let go of Jacob. But horror of horrors, Jacob fell right down into the chimney!

Little Bear started to cry. That's what you do when your best friend has just fallen down a chimney.

"My name is Herr Ermenrich," said the stork.

That didn't make Little Bear feel one bit better.

"Fragile monkeys are very unusual around here," said Herr Ermenrich.

Jacob falls down the chimney

"So, naturally, I thought he was a frog. Now I'll save him."

Little Bear just covered his eyes with his paws and cried, while Herr Ermenrich took the rug in his beak and leaned down into the chimney. Little Bear had to stop crying and hold on to Herr Ermenrich's feet. The plan was for him to hand the rug down to Jacob, so he could climb up on it.

But just then Little Bear sneezed and lost both his balance and his hold on Herr Ermenrich's feet. Down into the chimney went first the rug, then Herr Ermenrich, and last of all Little Bear.

"Jacob, are you there?" asked Little Bear.

"No," said Jacob in a weak voice. "I'm not sure. Where am I?"

"Inside Glimminge Castle," said Herr Ermenrich.

"It's dark in here," said Jacob, from under the rug.

"This is a very strong castle," said Herr Ermenrich. "It was built almost five hundred years ago. No enemy has ever managed to break in."

"Has anyone ever managed to break out?" asked Little Bear.

"Good question," said Herr Ermenrich.

Then all three of them crawled out of the gigantic fireplace where they had landed. Through a chink in the wall, they could see it was getting light outside.

"We have to get home before Christina wakes up," said Little Bear.

They went all the way downstairs to the ground floor.

"The sun will be coming up soon," said Little Bear, worried, as they stood in front of the huge locked door.

Herr Ermenrich threw back his head and made a click with his beak.

Instantly, someone on the other side answered by blowing on a small reed flute. Then there was a rattling in the lock. With all their strength, they pushed until they managed to open the enormously heavy door.

On the doorstep stood an unusually small boy wearing wooden shoes and a stocking cap. He was actually no bigger than a hand.

"I presume," said Herr Ermenrich, "that you are Herr Holgersson, first name Nils. This is Herr Little Bear and Herr Jacob. Due to one thing and another, we happened to fall down the chimney."

"I can see that," said Nils Holgersson. "You are all terribly sooty."

"And I'm not even washable," said Jacob.

"But the rug must be," said Herr Ermenrich. "And you certainly aren't thinking of flying on such a filthy rug."

"No," said Little Bear. "Christina might suspect something if we did."

24

So they went to a nearby moat and washed the rug. But guess what. Afterward, when Little Bear said the verse, the rug wouldn't fly.

"May I be of any help?" asked Herr Ermenrich. "I could fly you the first part of your journey, dragging the rug behind me. It would dry in the wind."

"Isn't Nils Holgersson coming with us?" asked Little Bear.

*Jacob and Little Bear
on Herr Ermenrich's back*

"No, thanks. I'll take a goose, instead," said Nils Holgersson.

They had to hold on tight, because Herr Ermenrich flew much faster than the rug. When they were about halfway, they said goodbye and got back on the rug.

"How are we going to make it in time?" asked Little Bear. "Christina wakes up in ten minutes. We should have taken the stork all the way."

"Hux flux pabulumlusk," said Jacob.

And believe it or not, even though he said it wrong as usual, the rug started to pick up speed.

"Maybe that's because it was just washed," said Little Bear.

"I don't think that's it at all," said Jacob.

In the end, the rug flew so terribly fast that Little Bear and Jacob had to lie on their stomachs to keep from blowing off. And then they were almost home. They could see the lights …

And *just* before Christina woke up, the rug swished in through the window and landed on her bedroom floor. Quick as a wink, Little Bear and Jacob climbed up in bed and snuggled down under the covers.

Just then, Christina woke up.

Jacob and Little Bear back in bed again

25

Selma and Us

ome years later, Christina's father read aloud to her from a Swedish book called *The Wonderful Adventures of Nils*. It was written by Selma Lagerlöf. Christina thought the story was much too sad. You never could be too sure of what would happen in any chapter. Suddenly someone would just die. And let's not even talk about the ending: oh, how Christina cried when the wild geese left Nils Holgersson.

The Wonderful Adventures of Nils

But in one of the chapters Nils visited Glimminge Castle and met Herr Ermenrich!

"How strange," said Christina. "Little Bear and Jacob also met Herr Ermenrich. Has Selma Lagerlöf copied Little Bear and Jacob?"

"No," said her father. "I think it's more likely it was the other way around."

Uncle Ragnar (seven) and Christina's dad (two)

Selma Lagerlöf was Christina's father's idol. He had all her books. When he was little, his mother painted a portrait of Selma. (His mother was an artist.) Selma had to come to their house for the sittings. When she left, Christina's dad and his brother, Ragnar, would rush in to try to be first to sit in the chair Selma had just sat in. That was because she was famous and had even won the Nobel Prize.

When Christina learned to write, she began writing her own stories. At school, it was called "writing compositions."

"I wonder what you'll be when you grow up," said

Selma Lagerlöf as Grandma (Kerstin Lundberg) painted her in 1918

Christina's father. "Since you like writing so much, you could become an author. How nice it would be if you became another Selma Lagerlöf."

"No. Never in my life would I want to write such sad stories," said Christina. "Besides, I'm going to be a trapeze artist in the circus."

Later she changed her mind and wanted to be a tap dancer in Hollywood. In the end, she became a story writer, but not exactly another Selma Lagerlöf, of course; that was a bit too much to ask.

Christina's mother (at seven)

Christina's Mother's Story

 I remember one time, when Christina's father was bicycling around the countryside trying to track down his ancestors, Christina told her mother that she needed to hear a Little Bear and Jacob story before she could fall asleep.

"Oh no, *I'm* not the one who can make up stories," her mother said. "But I can read a little *Heidi* to you."

Heidi was another sad story (in two volumes) which Christina's mother had from when she was little. They would both cry when they read it. It was worse than *The Wonderful Adventures of Nils*.

Heidi

"No, not *Heidi*," said Christina. "Tell a Little Bear and Jacob story. It's easy. Here's what you do:

"Just when Christina had fallen asleep, Little Bear and Jacob climbed down to the rug, and Little Bear said: '*Abracadabra, misinka misoo, sibbeday sibbido, extra lara, Kathy Klara, rug bug pabulum-ugh, out with you, my long long MAN!*' And just then the rug flew out the window … (And now you say where it flew.)"

"But I don't know how," said Christina's mother.

"*Try,*" said Christina.

So her mother tried. First the rug wandered this way and that over the city, around City Hall and Kronoberg Park. Then it took off toward Uncle Ragnar's apartment house.

Uncle Ragnar had two exciting things in his apartment house that Christina didn't have in hers (hers was much too old). He had an *elevator* and a *garbage chute*.

Little Bear and Jacob got into the elevator and stood up on a chair they pulled down from the wall, so they could see themselves in the mirror. Then Little Bear jumped up and pushed the highest button, so the elevator went up to the top floor. They got out there and went over to the garbage chute. It wasn't easy to open the lid, but Little Bear finally managed to do it. Then they both jumped in and slid down the fantastic garbage chute. Their stomachs tickled like mad, but it was so much fun they kept riding the elevator up and the garbage chute down almost all night long. They got all covered with potato peels and anchovy bones.

Then Jacob wanted to push the button (even though Little Bear already had), and Jacob pushed the *red* button by mistake, and the elevator came to a full stop! Little Bear and Jacob jumped up and down, pushing all the buttons, but the elevator wouldn't budge.

Finally Uncle Ragnar woke up and wondered what the racket out in the hall was all about. He came out in his striped pajamas. Just as he managed to save Little Bear and Jacob, his own door slammed shut! And there was Uncle Ragnar in his striped pajamas, locked out of his apartment, standing with Little Bear and Jacob, and there was a horrible stench of anchovies.

Then Little Bear took the rug and flew out, and up, and in through Uncle Ragnar's window (which was open), and unlocked the door.

At that moment Uncle Ragnar's alarm clock went off, and Little Bear shouted, "Oh no, Christina will be waking up! Come on, Jacob, we have to go."

And then it was *abracadabra* and all the rest, and off they went home, in through the window, and up into Christina's bed, just as she woke up.

So Christina's mother *could* make up stories. She just hadn't ever *tried* before.

*Jacob
and Little Bear
back in bed again*

Christina still has the rug. It's red and white, crocheted, with a red fringe. They go together, Christina and that rug. They still share the same room. But the rug is so old now it can't fly anymore. At least, that's what Christina thinks. But how does she know; she is always asleep when …

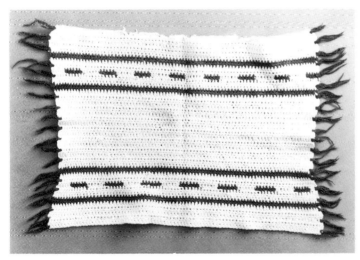

The rug

Christina

Cousin Jan (Uncle Ragnar's son), who, when he grew up, invented a forklift for the teddy bears and the teddy-bear film (see pages 64–65)

Middleword

 had gotten this far when Christina came and started reading through what I had written.

"So," she said, "is this how it's going to be? I don't think this is what I had in mind for the teddy-bear book."

"Hmm," I said. "What do you mean?"

"You keep getting sidetracked," said Christina. "Do you think people find it interesting to read about Selma Lagerlöf and things like that?"

"I can't be bothered with that," I said. "I can only write about things *I* find interesting."

"But," said Christina, "what about all the other things that were supposed to be in the book: the teddy bears' history, famous teddy bears, teddy bears in England, all of that?"

"Don't worry," I said. "That comes later."

"And that chapter," said Christina, "about why people love teddy bears?"

"Listen, Christina," I said. "Of course people love teddy bears. You don't even need to write that down."

"Well, but I just thought that maybe …"

"Put it in at the end, then, as an afterword, with a warning first," I said. "But I'm not going to write it. On the other hand, I *am* going to write about the time I went with you to the doctor."

"Oh yes, do!" said Christina. "That was really important."

Christina and I Go to the Doctor

Sometimes Christina had to go to the doctor. Either she had whooping cough or swollen glands or she just needed to get an immunization. I usually went along as support.

I especially remember one time when she was going to get an immunization — for diphtheria, maybe. First we sat for a while in the waiting room. There were toys there, mostly trucks and things Christina wasn't so interested in. (Were they the doctor's toys, or his children's?) We weren't in the mood for playing.

A nurse came out and said, "Christina Lundberg, this way, please."

Christina thought it was completely unnecessary to be immunized.

But then the doctor said, "All right, then, we'll start with the teddy bear. What's his name?"

"Big Bear," said Christina.

"He certainly is big," said the doctor. "Such a big bear wouldn't be afraid of a little shot."

What could I do? I had to be brave so Christina would see there was nothing to be afraid of.

"My teddy-bear needle, please," said the doctor.

The nurse wiped off my leg with a cotton ball soaked in alcohol. Then the doctor stuck the needle right into my leg. I remember the crunching sound in my excelsior stuffing.

Because I had been so brave, Christina had to be brave, too. When her turn came, the

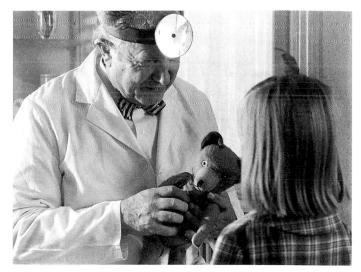

From a film about our trip to the doctor (see pages 64–65)

nurse wiped her leg with a cotton ball. Then came the needle (no crunching sound at all for Christina). Finally the nurse dried her leg with another cotton ball.

"Dry Big Bear, too," said Christina.

The Cast

**R**iding on a hay wagon one summer, Christina fell off. As she lay there in the field, she saw that her arm looked like a Z. Oh no, how awful! She cried all the way to the hospital. Luckily, Little Bear was with her.

At the hospital the doctor said her arm was *broken, in two places.* That made Christina even more frightened. She thought she had broken her arm not only where it hurt but *some other place,* too. The doctor meant she had broken two bones in her arm.

Then he put Christina and Little Bear to sleep with ether (ether is the worst thing in the world) and set Christina's arm. Afterward, they had to stay at the hospital. But the arm didn't heal right, so the doctor had to put Christina and Little Bear to sleep *again* with that terrible ether. Then he put in splints to make sure the bone would grow together correctly this time. Around her arm he put a plaster cast that went from her hand all the way up to her shoulder. Christina and Little Bear had to stay in the hospital for several weeks (or maybe it was days; Little Bear doesn't remember).

What a nasty scar   By fall, the arm was healed, and Christina and I went to the doctor again.

"Now we'll get rid of this cast," the doctor told Christina.

That made Christina unhappy; she had become very fond of her cast. It was like a part of her. In the end the doctor had to let her take it home, but only after she promised to use it only in an emergency.

For years the cast lay in a closet. After a while, Christina had grown so much she couldn't get it on anymore. Then it disappeared; I don't remember how.

Christina still has the scar on her arm. Just look what an ugly job of sewing that doctor did.

If the War Comes to Sweden

During Christina's childhood, World War II started. Sweden, where she lived, wasn't part of the fighting, but all the other countries around Sweden were. Christina didn't notice the war so much, except when the news came on the radio in the living room and she wasn't allowed to talk. She didn't want to hear about that awful war and how the Germans took one country after another and dropped bombs. How strange. Were they Grandma's relatives? (Grandma was born German.)

Huggy Yellow holding on to the coupons

During the war, everyone had to have ration cards with small coupons in order to buy food. When you used up all your butter coupons, you weren't allowed to buy more butter until you got your new ration cards for the next month. There were coupons for shoes and clothes, but not for teddy bears.

In our room, we rationed all kinds of things. Christina played with some old ration cards she got from Grandma. They had "expired." (That meant they were too old to be used; they were from *World War I.*)

"Remember, they're called *coupons*," Christina would tell us. "Not *poohpons* like little kids say."

Huggy Yellow got a special little wallet to put our coupons in.

"Now, don't lose the coupons," Christina told Huggy Yellow sternly. "That's the worst thing you could lose; it's better to lose money."

There would not be war in Sweden; that's what Per Albin said. He was Prime Minister of Sweden. But just think if a bomb dropped on Pipers Street, anyway. That had happened once. It wasn't a war bomb but a bomb some crook had planted in a taxi. The bomb had gone off on Pipers Street.

Just to be on the safe side, Christina took all of us teddy bears and put us in a hatbox that she hid in the closet. She put in some crayons, and a flashlight, and some money and coupons, too. (She had gotten millions of old German marks from Grandma.) Then, if there was an air raid, she could just grab the hatbox and dash downstairs to the shelter in the basement.

Christina didn't tell anyone she had us in the closet. That proved to be a good idea for another reason, too. I'll tell you about that now.

The Adventure in the Closet

Sometimes, when Christina had been naughty, she was punished by being locked in the closet. For example, there was the time she broke *"J'attendrai"* (her father's favorite record), or when she drew on the wallpaper; then she went straight to the closet. What luck the hatbox was in there! (And that there was a light!) Christina had a great time with us in the closet. One time her father discovered the light, and after that, she wasn't allowed to turn it on. That's when the flashlight came in handy. And if she was mad at her parents, Christina could always take out the crayons and draw on the closet wall (but only *behind* the clothes or *under* the shoe shelf).

When they came and asked if she had gotten nice yet, Christina would say, "No, not yet."

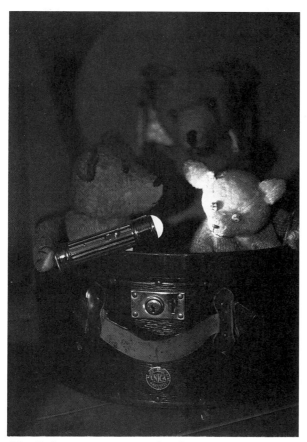

The lights were supposed to be out in the closet

That was because she wanted to try on her mother's silver shoes, the ones with the enormous high heels. But later, when the dumb flashlight batteries would run out, she was glad to come out.

It was lucky that neither Christina nor any of us teddy bears were really afraid in there. These days nobody locks kids in closets (I don't think so, anyway), but many parents didn't know any better back then.

For us teddy bears, the time-out in the closet was probably good practice for the really dark times to come. But I'll get to that later on in this book. (Although it will take quite a while.)

The Big Flood

Monica was twenty-two days older than Christina. They lived in the same building on Pipers Street, but Monica's entrance was on another street. It was a lot closer to get to Monica's apartment by going through the attic. There were no lights up there and it was pitch-dark, so it was lucky that neither Monica nor Christina was the least bit afraid of the dark. The only thing they needed to be worried about was fish. One time Monica's grandma had soaked some dried fish up in the attic, and left a whole pailful standing out in the hallway. In the dark, Christina had tripped over it and *almost* fallen in.

Christina and Monica had a secret place high up on some boards under the attic ceiling. It was wonderful and forbidden to be up there, especially when they opened the rooftop window to look out over the whole city ...

Other than that, Christina liked playing at home best (with us teddy bears). At Monica's there were only dolls and board games and playing cards. Christina thought board games were really boring.

Sometimes Monica would say, "I'm the one who decides, because I'm older."

Then Christina had to go up and play at Monica's. But on this particular day they were at Christina's, drinking hot chocolate. There was even enough for us teddy bears. Christina put bibs on us, and Monica set our little table with doll dishes. Then they poured hot chocolate into all the cups. Christina made sure that she was the one to serve the smallest teddy bears. Their cups were so tiny you almost had to stop pouring before you started, or else the hot chocolate would run over.

"Drink. Drink," said Monica, holding the cup in front of my snout.

"Not *really*," said Christina, nervously.

"My dolls always *really* drink," said Monica.

Christina (1) and (Monica (2) in first grade, two years after the flood

"Yes, because they're washable," said Christina. "They're hard."

"Look," said Monica. "He drank it all up!"

She showed Christina my empty cup. Actually, I had seen Monica take a drink from my cup herself, while Christina was filling the little teddy-bear cups. I was lucky I got only a tiny bit of hot chocolate on my snout. Christina dried it off with my bib.

When we were all done, it was time to do the dishes. There was a sink with running water behind a little door in Christina's room. She and Monica each stood on a stool, so they could reach up to the sink and wash the dishes.

Suddenly Monica filled the tiniest cup with water and threw it on Christina's hair. Christina did the same thing to Monica, of course. They did it over and over. Then they used bigger cups … Some water ended up on the floor.

After a while they were using the biggest doll cups. They were laughing so hard they almost fell off their stools. We sat there at our table and watched the water start running in small streams across the floor. Soon it had reached our table.

Then Christina and Monica found a water pitcher they could use to pour water on the floor. It's too bad I have such floppy legs. The other teddy bears' legs always stick straight out when they sit, but mine hang down from the chair. Oh no! Now my paws were getting soaked!

Just when the whole floor was flooded, Christina's mother walked in.

"Mein Gott!" she cried. (German for "My God!") *"What* are you doing?"

"We're just playing," said Christina.

And then it occurred to her that this was something they probably weren't allowed to do. Christina's mother put on her rubber boots and started scooping up the water into a bucket with a dustpan.

"Stay where you are!" she hissed at Christina and Monica up on their stools. "Which one of you started this?"

"Neither of us," said Christina. She knew it wasn't nice to tattle.

"We started with just the *tiniest* little bit," said Monica.

When most of the water was cleaned up, Monica borrowed some dry clothes from Christina. Then Christina's mother took Monica home and told her grandmother how naughty the girls had been.

I don't know how Monica was punished, but Christina had to undress and go to bed right in the middle of the day. That was worse than being locked in the closet. Then Christina's mother called her father at work and told not only him but also Mrs. Straube, the switchboard operator.

When Christina's father came home, he was very angry with her. The floor was still wet in spots. He went downstairs to talk to Aunt Ingrid, who lived in the apartment under us, and he saw that there were small wet stains on her ceiling. When he came back upstairs, he was so mad he had those half-closed eyes that we hated. Now Christina got a new punishment: her father didn't speak to her all evening. There wasn't even a chance for a bedtime story.

Now, Christina could understand that pouring water out on the floor was naughty, because she had done it on purpose; that's why she was sent to bed. But she had never *meant* for the water to leak down into Aunt Ingrid's apartment, so I don't think it was fair of Christina's father to punish her again.

The next morning everything was back to normal — except for my paws, which were still damp.

Now, when Christina thinks about the Great Flood, what she remembers is how much fun she and Monica had, pouring out all that water. It had been exciting to see how much they could dump out on the floor. So maybe it was worth all the punishment that came later. Or maybe not.

Soon the water had reached all the way to my paws ...

Teddy Bears Are Good to Take Along

At times, Christina had to go away. That was when her mother was sick, or else when she was so well that she was able to go along on one of Christina's father's business trips to Paris. I don't know what business trips are, but it was something they did out of the country.

Christina had the most fun when she went to Gothenburg and stayed with her cousin Birgitta and the yaiyas. The yaiyas were Birgitta's teddy bears (she had as least as many as Christina) and a stuffed dog named Old Man, who fell in the toilet one time.

Giant Yaiya today

Christina would have liked to take all of us teddy bears with her, but she wasn't allowed to. Little Bear and Jacob always got to go; sometimes Baby Snow White, Baby Yellow, and I did, too.

Birgitta's biggest teddy bear was called Giant Yaiya. Before I met him, I thought I was probably the biggest teddy bear in the world, but Giant Yaiya was *much* bigger. He could wear Christina's old dress, he was that big.

Sometimes Birgitta and some of the yaiyas came to Stockholm to visit Christina. Then we would stay up all night playing — Christina, Birgitta, the yaiyas, and all of us teddy bears. Christina's parents didn't notice anything until we started roller skating.

Other times Christina stayed with her cousins Christopher and Johan, who lived in Stockholm. That

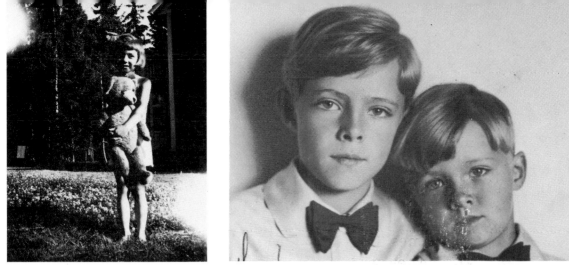

Birgitta and Giant Yaiya, 1944

Chris and Johan

was fun, too. Christina pretended that Chris and Johan were her big brothers. She decided that, when she grew up, she would marry Johan (but it never happened). Chris had a pink teddy bear that was blind. It came from Czechoslovakia. But Chris played mostly with his tin soldiers.

Johan played with Christina, or with a red bus made of cast iron. I think maybe he had a blue cat, too. I know that he had three imaginary playmates: Mimmi, Gnangbull, and Polaydos. Christina didn't have any imaginary playmates, but when Little Bear got his new fur covering, she got a little piece that was left over. She named it Mimmi, after Johan's Mimmi, and kept it under her pillow. Later, when she got another piece of fur, she pretended it was Mimmi's Aunt Moma.

Chris's teddy bear today

Once, when Chris and Johan had chicken pox, Christina had to stay with Aunt Inez, instead. Little Bear and Mimmi and Moma went with her. Unfortunately, Christina got a cold and Aunt Inez put her to bed.

"The girl is obviously allergic to cat fur," said Aunt Inez. "It must be that nasty old fur teddy bear that's giving her such a runny nose."

That was all wrong. Christina wasn't allergic to Little Bear! But Aunt Inez took him away and put him in a cabinet. You can just imagine how sad that made Christina! She had never slept without Little Bear in her whole life. Not even Mimmi and Moma (whom Aunt Inez hadn't found) were able to comfort her.

Do Teddy Bears Go to Heaven?

I remember one time when we all had colds. Mrs. Peters (who helped Christina's mother clean house) was baby-sitting, because Christina's parents were visiting Grandma in the hospital. Suddenly Mrs. Peters came in and said that Grandma was dead.

"Dead?" said Christina. "Why is she dead?"

"It was *angina pectoris*," said Mrs. Peters.

"When is Grandma coming home?" Christina asked.

"She's never coming home again," said Mrs. Peters.

Christina thought at that time that Angina Pectoris was a witch who had taken Grandma away. But that was wrong; angina is a heart disease that had made Grandma's heart stop. That's why she died. Mrs. Peters showed how Grandma looked, lying there dead in the hospital, with her eyes closed.

When Christina's father came home, we knew how really serious it was, because he was crying. We had never seen him cry before. Christina's mother cried sometimes (when she lost her ration coupons or something). And Christina cried when she fell down and hurt herself. But her father never cried.

"Where's Grandma?" asked Christina.

"She's in heaven," said her father.

"Mrs. Peters says she's in the hospital," said Christina.

"That's only her body," said her father. "Her soul is in heaven. We won't be able to see Grandma anymore."

Grandma came from Germany

"Never?" sobbed Christina.

"Not as long as we are alive," said her father. "But when we die, we'll go to heaven, too. Then maybe we'll see Grandma."

There was no bedtime story that night. Everybody was too sad. We lay there in bed thinking about heaven and wondering what it was like. It must be a little like being in church, Christina thought, but with clouds and no roof.

Suddenly Christina thought of something important. She called out to her father.

"Am I going to heaven when I die?" she asked.

"Yes, that's what I just said," answered her father.

"But can teddy bears go to heaven?" asked Christina. "Because if teddy bears can't go to heaven, then I don't want to go, either."

"Well, I think it's like this," said her father. "Everyone who has a soul can go to heaven. People all have souls, and so do animals."

"But do teddy bears have souls?" asked Christina.

"Probably not from the beginning," said her father. "Not when you first buy them. But now your teddy bears each have a little soul, because you've played with them and loved them so much that you've given them a little bit of *your* soul."

"Oh," said Christina. "That's good!"

Then we lay there a long time in the dark, talking about heaven, all of us.

"In the front row of heaven sit all the people," said Christina. "And Uncle Harry is there playing the organ. A little farther back are the monkeys and dogs and pigs and that squirrel that got run over. Then there are the birds and the mosquitoes. And way in the back are all the teddy bears ..."

Uncle Harry (Lindgren) at the organ in Klara Church, Stockholm

UP IN HEAVEN

*At that time
Christina thought
that heaven
probably looked
like this*

Crowded in Bed

 fter a while, Christina thought it wasn't fair that only Little Bear and Jacob got to sleep in her bed, and she decided that all of us should sleep with her. When her father came in to tell her a story, he got worried.

"You can't have your bed this crowded," he said.

"It's not crowded," said Christina.

"Yes, it is," said her father. "There's not even enough room for you. Let me take away the biggest ones, anyway, Big Bear and Teddy Yellow."

"No!" said Christina. "Teddy Yellow gets to sleep closest to me tonight, because he slept at the edge last night."

Christina was very particular about where we slept. It was especially important where Teddy Yellow slept, since he was the newest. Otherwise, he might think that Christina didn't love him as much as she loved her old teddy bears. Well, did she? Christina didn't even dare think about such things.

From the film Teddy Bears and People *that Christina and Maria Brännström made. Christina and her father were played by actors, but we teddy bears played ourselves.*

It ended up that all of us were allowed to sleep together.

"Now I'll turn off the light," said her father after the story.

"No, wait. Baby Yellow is lost," said Christina.

We all looked for him, even under the mattress. When we finally found him, Christina's father got to turn out the light.

But when she woke up the next morning, Christina saw the strangest thing: only Little Bear and Jacob were still in bed. The rest of us were already up and sitting in our little doll chairs …

We Go to a Museum

 ometimes I got to go with Christina and her father to a museum. Once in a while Christina's mother went with us, too, when she was feeling well enough to walk.

At the amusement park

"Guess which museum we're going to today," Christina asked me one Sunday.

"The amusement park," I said.

"That's no museum," said Christina. "A museum is a place where they put a lot of things that you can go look at. If the things are ancient, then it's a historical museum; if they're pictures, it's an art museum; if they're animals, it's the Museum of Natural History."

"Or the zoo," I said.

Jacob used to go with us to the zoo to visit the monkeys in the monkey house. Christina asked her father if the zoo was a museum. He said yes, it was an outdoor museum.

But today it was the Museum of Natural History, and I got to go along. Mostly we looked at the stuffed brown bear. It wasn't in a glass case, so we could pat its fur. We skipped the whales, because they smelled so bad. But we saw the sun bear, the proboscis monkey, and lots of other animals.

Christina's father said that at midnight all the animals in the museum came alive. Christina wanted to stay until then, but her father said we couldn't, because the museum closed at four o'clock.

Christina thought we ought to stay, anyway. We could sleep up on top of the brown bear and wake up when he came alive.

That night Christina's father told about what happened when Little Bear and Jacob flew to the Museum of Natural History on their rug. At midnight. Unfortunately, I don't have room to tell that story here, but you can just imagine ...

Outside the zoo (free admission for anyone dressed in national costume)

Midnight at the Museum of Natural History ...

The Arrival of Winnie-the-Pooh

(A literary chapter)

How strange that neither Christina nor I can remember when we got *Winnie-the-Pooh*. Christina had gotten *Pippi Longstocking* for her birthday when she was eight, in the summer of 1946 (what a great book that is), but didn't we already have *Pooh* then?

Christina's father was the one who'd discovered it at Cousin Birgitta's house, when he was reading her a story. Right then, he decided we had to have the book, too.

Christina's father would read us one chapter each night. All the chapters had long names. For example:

CHAPTER III
In Which
Pooh and Piglet Go Hunting
and Nearly Catch a Woozle

We wondered a lot about what that *"In Which"* could mean.

The best thing about Pooh was that he and all his friends lived out in the forest. We wanted to do that, too. We used to pretend that Christina's room was a forest and that we each lived in our own tree. Christina had

a green door on hers, just like Christopher Robin.

Imagine. They had a whole *world of their own* out in the forest. Christina thought all books should be about your own world. The ordinary world wasn't nearly as much fun.

We liked that Pooh, who was a Bear of Very Little Brain, could often understand things better than wise Owl and know-it-all Rabbit. But it was Piglet who was Christina's favorite. She often felt as unsure of herself as Piglet did. That's why it was so wonderful when he'd do something *really brave* every now and then.

We liked the pictures in the book a lot. But the strange thing was that at that time the bear on the cover wasn't Pooh; the other bear looked silly. But whoever it was who had drawn the real Pooh, the one inside the book, he was the best artist in the whole world, said Christina. Even if the pictures were small, and you could see only a little bit of the forest, you knew *exactly* how it looked. And how Owl's house was. And Piglet! He was so cute that we would get tears in our eyes sometimes.

Pooh looks silly on the cover, says Baby Snow White

When the last chapter was finished, and Christopher Robin had dragged Pooh upstairs — bump, bump, bump — everything felt so empty. Christina's father had to read the book over and over, but even that didn't really help.

"It can't just end there," said Christina. "There's got to be some more."

Her father looked into the matter, which wasn't all that hard to do. On the back of the book it said:

BONNIERS CHILDREN'S LIBRARY. *In this series, aimed at boys and girls six to ten years old, offering classic as well as new high-quality, entertaining children's books at the low price of 2 crowns, are the following:*

And then there was a list of seventy-four books. *Winnie-the-Pooh* was number 4. Guess what was number 18? *The House at Pooh Corner*! Luckily, Christina's father had two crowns, and so he bought it for us right away. It was just as good as the first book!

By now Christina had learned to read, so she could read *The House at Pooh Corner* herself. She was so afraid the book would end that she read each chapter several times. Espe-

cially Chapter VIII, *"In Which* Piglet Does a Very Grand Thing."* We knew *exactly* how the wind would have blown that day to make Piglet's ears stream behind him like banners ...

Christina finally had to come to the last chapter: *"In Which* Christopher Robin and Pooh Come to an Enchanted Place, and We Leave Them There." Oh, it was so terribly sad. We cried every time. And it really was enchanted. All books should have enchanted places, said Christina, the kind that give you butterflies in your stomach and make you take a deep breath.

But the worst part was that the end was *impossible* to understand. The chapter started like this:

Christopher Robin was going away. Nobody knew why he was going; nobody knew where he was going; indeed, nobody even knew why he knew that Christopher Robin was going away. But somehow or other everybody in the Forest felt that it was happening at last. Even Smallest-of-All, a friend-and-relation of Rabbit's who thought he had once seen Christopher Robin's foot, but couldn't be sure because perhaps it was something else, even S.-of-A. told himself that Things were going to be Different ...

There we all sat, as sad as could be. First of all, the book was finished; Pooh and the others were leaving us. And if that weren't enough, Christopher Robin was leaving *them*! Everything would change. Why? Was it really necessary?

We comforted ourselves by thinking there would probably be a third Pooh book that would explain everything. In the meantime, Christina stopped at the library on the way home from school. I didn't get to go with her any longer, since it was unthinkable to take a teddy bear with you to school. She borrowed one after another of the books listed on the back of *Winnie-the-Pooh,* but none of them was anywhere near as good.

Why couldn't it be like this forever?

One time Christina just happened to take down a big dark blue book from the library shelf. It was called *The Wind in the Willows*. When she opened it up, Christina saw that the pictures were like the ones in *Winnie-the-Pooh*. Finally, she thought, I've found the third Pooh book, only they've made this one a little bigger!

But it wasn't true. Neither Pooh nor Piglet was in this book. It was about a rat and a mole and a badger and a toad. And it wasn't the same forest. A. A. Milne hadn't written it, but someone named Kenneth Grahame. The pictures, however, were drawn by E. H. Shepard, the person who illustrated *Winnie-the-Pooh* (although they forgot to write that in the first Pooh book).

It turned out that *The Wind in the Willows* was as good as *Winnie-the-Pooh* (well, almost as good). It had its own world, with several enchanted places. One chapter was called "The Piper at the Gates of Dawn." It always made Christina take a deep breath. She didn't really understand all of it, but it didn't matter, because it *felt* enchanted. But she usually skipped over the chapters about Mr. Toad's adventures.

*Mole's forest was
as fine as Pooh's …*

The Piper at the Gates of Dawn

The years went by. Unfortunately, no new *Pooh* book came out. But we did find out, finally, why Christopher Robin had to leave Pooh and the others, and where he went. That's coming up later in this book. Don't think everything has been said about Pooh.

Putte-Malajjo from Celle

uddenly Christina was twelve years old. That summer, her father decided that she should visit her grandmother's relatives in Germany. Luckily, the war was over by now.

Christina had to travel alone by train, which she thought was really scary, even though Little Bear went with her, and a monkey named Rebecca, and Rebecca's two small daughters, Diana and Misma. They could see that the war must have been horrible; almost every town the train passed through had been bombed. Sometimes there wasn't a single house left standing, only ruins.

Christina got off in Hamburg, where she visited the Hagenbeck Zoo with some other Swedish children who had been with her on the train. Hamburg had been bombed, but not the zoo (as far as Christina could see).

All too soon, Christina had to say goodbye to the Swedish children and continue on to the little town of Celle. Even though her relatives lived in the prettiest little half-timbered house (which hadn't been bombed), it wasn't any fun there. Christina could speak Swedish and English, but the only German she knew was "Mein Gott," and her relatives didn't speak any Swedish or English. Thanks to Little Bear and Rebecca, she survived the three weeks.

Putte-Malajjo. The gentlemen in the background are members of the Södertälje Swim Club

The most fun Christina had in Celle was finding Putte-Malajjo in a toy store. He was a little sun bear (*Helarctos malayanus,* in Latin) and cost most of Christina's allowance, but he was worth it.

"What does that little metal button on your ear mean?" we asked Putte-Malajjo when they came home.

"It means Steiff," said Putte-Malajjo.

"And what does Steiff mean?"

"Incredibly strong," said Putte-Malajjo.

Putte-Malajjo in Celle (on Rebecca's lap, in the middle)

Christina says that's not right; Steiff is only the name of a factory. But they make really good teddy bears there, and Putte-Malajjo is really strong. He may have been my son, maybe not. Christina wasn't so particular about such things any longer. I think she was starting to grow up and move away from us …

Christina Starts Collecting Monkeys

It wasn't good that Christina was growing up. The bigger she got, the smaller we became. She didn't play with us as often any longer. And then the *monkeys* arrived.

"I've met Jacob's grandfather Abraham," Christina's father wrote on a postcard from Brussels, when he was there on a business trip.

When her father traveled to another country, he always brought Christina a monkey: Isaac came from Madrid, Manasseh from Rome, Joseph from Paris. They were all related to each other and had Old Testament names.

The amazing thing was that when Christina started secondary school she had a classmate who also collected monkeys. Her name was Ulla. Christina and Ulla starting having monkey parties, one after another. They ordered Black Forest cakes and had a lovely time. We teddy bears were never invited. Sometimes Clumsy Bear got to come; that was Ulla's only teddy bear. Christina and Ulla said if all of Christina's teddy bears were invited to the parties, it would be too crowded.

The monkeys, 1951

We teddy bears didn't have anything against monkeys, except that Christina put us up on a shelf. And it got worse …

We End Up in the Attic

Ulla and Christina continued with the monkey parties for several years, while their classmates were starting to wear nylon stockings and learn to dance. Christina and Ulla didn't need to learn the waltz and fox-trot, because they were going to be Hollywood dancers. That's why they took tap-dancing lessons, instead. In Hollywood they would meet Gene Kelly, the famous dancer, and be invited to Esther Williams's house for a swim in her pool. They practiced swimming underwater, smiling the whole time, the way Esther Williams did in her movies.

Their classmates thought Christina and Ulla were too childish to belong to their dance club. But Christina finally managed to be invited to a party at her new friend Annika's. After that, she had no time for either monkeys or teddy bears. She had to wash her hair and do her nails and sew new clothes. We all got put back in the hatbox and ended up in the closet again (except for Little Bear). We didn't even get to come out when Christina graduated.

A few years later, Christina married one of her classmates and moved away from home. At that point, the hatbox ended up in the attic. Little Bear was the only one who got to go with Christina to her new home. However, he didn't get to sleep in Christina's bed but in a dresser drawer.

The next several years we spent inside the hatbox, but finally it just got *too* dull. One day we lifted the lid. I remember that Teddy Yellow and I pushed as hard as we could. We looked around.

Ulla and Christina tap dancing

Some light streamed in through a skylight.

"Look, there's our furniture!" said Huggy Yellow. "What good luck …"

"Good luck! It's more like bad luck to end up in the attic …" said Taxi Wollmar (Christina's oilcloth dachshund, who was also in the hatbox).

Teddy Yellow thought we should definitely climb out, but I said, "Teddy bears, I suggest we stay put in the hatbox, because Christina will be here soon to take us out."

The others didn't think so. So we climbed out, anyway, and arranged our furniture, and made it as cozy as we could for ourselves. We caught a glimpse of Christina's mother's old doll Goldie, on a shelf farther back in the attic, but we never did make any contact with her.

We lift the cover

Every time someone put a key in the lock to the attic door, I thought it might be Christina. But it never was.

I Give a Lecture

Everybody needed to be cheered up, so one day I volunteered to give a lecture.

"A lecture?" said Huggy Yellow. "What's that?"

"A lecture," I said, "is when you sit and listen, and I lecture. I talk. About something interesting. But maybe you don't want me to give a lecture."

"Of course we do," said Huggy Yellow.

"Actually, it all depends on what the lecture's about," said Taxi Wollmar.

"Today I had planned to talk about the history of the teddy bear," I said.

"Wake me when it's over," said Taxi Wollmar, who thought we talked too much about teddy bears and too little about dogs.

I pretended not to hear him, and started my lecture:

"At the turn of the century, some eighty to ninety years ago, there were no teddy bears ..."

"There have always been teddy bears," chirped Baby Snow White.

"Be quiet," said Teddy Yellow, "so we can hear."

Taxi Wollmar

The History of the Teddy Bear

"As I was saying," I said. "Around the year 1900 there were not yet any teddy bears. Children played with dolls. Girls, I mean. Boys played with tin soldiers, and trains, and wagons, and cannons. Nearly all toys were hard objects.

"Pay attention now! This is where the history of the teddy bear begins. The year is 1903, but it's all very mysterious. No one knows *exactly* how it happened, who it was who discovered the first teddy bear. The Americans say it was Morris Michtom from Brooklyn. In Germany, they say it was an old lady named Margarete Steiff ..."

"I'm cheering for Steiff," shouted Putte-Malajjo. "Steiff, Steiff! Go, Steiff, go!"

"In the town of Giengen, in the little Steiff family factory, Margarete, who sat in a wheelchair, had started making stuffed animals out of felt. Elephants and such. One day her nephew Richard visited the zoo and got an idea."

"What if we made a bear," he said.

"A bear?" said Margarete. "But bears look so dangerous."

Richard gave Margarete some drawings he had done of the brown bears in the zoo, and he asked her to try.

Margarete selected a furry fabric called mohair pile. She cut a bear shape out of it and sewed it. She tried to make her bear look as kind as possible, and she wanted him do more than just go on all fours; she made him able to stand upright and sit, too. To do that, Margarete had to make his arms and legs movable. Then she decided to make his head movable, too. The result was a cute little bear with a pointed nose and the slightly humped back that real brown bears have.

Richard Steiff took the bear with him to a big toy show in Leipzig. Most of the time it just lay there in a box; no one was particularly interested in a toy bear. What a strange doll, most of them thought. Then, on the last day, an American toy buyer came by. He was so charmed by Margarete's bear that he immediately ordered three thousand (3,000!) of them. The little factory in Giengen had to sew like crazy. When the three thousand bears were ready, they were shipped across the Atlantic to the United States.

Before there were teddy bears, children played with ...

... dolls ...

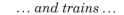

... and trains ...

... and carriages ...

... and tin soldiers ...

Margarete Steiff

The little factory in Giengen on the Brenz River

Margarete and her sister-in-law at the factory

This was in

1903

They made felt animals there, like this little elephant

Richard Steiff

Margarete had had polio and had to sit in a wheelchair

The first Steiff teddy bear

"Let's hope there wasn't a storm at sea," said Huggy Yellow. "I would get so seasick ..."

"But you weren't even there," said Teddy Yellow.

"Oh, that's right, I wasn't," said Huggy Yellow.

"The President of America — I mean the United States — at that time was named Theodore Roosevelt, but he was called Teddy. Once he went bear hunting. The only problem was no bears showed up, not for five days. The people who lived in the area thought that was so embarrassing that they caught a puny little bear and stood him up in front of the President.

"No, thanks," said President Teddy. "I'm not going to shoot that poor animal. That wouldn't be fair play. If I ever shot such a pitiful bear, I'd never be able to look my children in the eye again."

The newspapers found that remark so amazing they wrote about it for several days, and drew cartoons of Teddy Roosevelt and the bear. Long after that event, President Roosevelt was still drawn with a bear, even if it was to illustrate something completely different that he'd done.

One day in Brooklyn, New York, Morris Michtom stood in his little candy store reading the newspaper. His wife, Rose, made stuffed animals that they sold in the store. She made little ponies and such, but now Morris Michtom got an idea:

President Teddy Roosevelt   *Morris Michtom*   *The first Morris teddy bear*

56

"Why don't we make a bear," he said to Rose.

So they did. It so happened that it looked a lot like Margarete's bear. They displayed it in the store window, with a sign that said: TEDDY'S BEAR. The bear was sold immediately, and they had to make more.

Cartoons showing President Teddy Roosevelt and the bears

It occurred to Morris that the President might not like him calling the bears teddy bears. So he sent one of their bears to President Roosevelt, along with a letter asking if they could name the bears after him. The President gave the bear to his children, and wrote back to Morris, saying it was fine with him if he wanted to use the name *teddy bear.*

"What about Steiff?" Putte-Malajjo wondered. He was worried.

"Don't worry, " I said. "In Germany, they say that when those three thousand bears arrived in America, some of them were bought and used for table decorations at a wedding the President was invited to. And that's where they got the name *teddy bears."*

"Which story is right?" asked Teddy Yellow.

The sales curve for teddy bears rose sharply

974.000 st **1907**

1906

1903

3.000 st

An English girl (1910) and a Swedish boy (1915) with their teddy bears

"Nobody knows," I said. "There's no proof, since both Morris Michtom's and the President's letters are lost. And there's no one who remembers what actually happened at that wedding.

"The only thing we do know is that teddy bears became enormously popular. The Michtoms founded a giant toy company called Ideal Toys. They made a fortune with their teddy bears. The factory is still in business.

"And Steiff's factory had to expand. Teddy-bear sales increased every year. Several doll manufacturers were worried that they would go bankrupt; children all wanted teddy bears. That's what's so good about us teddy bears: both boys and girls like to play with us."

This is how many teddy bears the Steiff factory made in one day in 1907!

We Almost Get Stolen

 As we were sitting up in the attic as usual one night, trying to kill time, we heard a lot of rustling and banging at the attic door. Could that be Christina, in the middle of the night? No, it was two men who were forcing open the big steel door.

"Teddy bears, back in the hatbox!" I whispered.

By now the men were in the attic hallway, trying the doors to the different storage rooms. We were all back inside the hatbox. I was trying to close the lid, but it wasn't working. My heart was beating wildly!

Now they were right in front of our door! It was easy for them to break open the flimsy padlock and get in. They started digging through all the old skis and evening clothes.

"What a lot of junk," one of them said, looking at us in the hatbox. "But there's an antique," he said, stepping farther in and spotting Goldie.

"I know a guy who got ten grand for one of these old clocks," said the other.

And then they took off, with Goldie and Christina's beloved grandfather clock — the one that had belonged to her grandfather, and great-grandfather, and great-great-grandfather. Christina's father had written it all down for her inside the case.

What luck that the robbers thought *we* were just a lot of junk!

It was several weeks before Christina discovered there had been a robbery in the attic. In the meantime, all our doll furniture had disappeared: the sofa and table and chairs, the little red dresser, the doll bed that Chris and Johan had made for Christina, and our pretty piano.

"Just when I had decided to learn how to play," said Teddy Yellow.

 Imagine, people thought they could simply help themselves to whatever they wanted, just because the door was unlocked!

When Christina understood how *close* we came to being stolen, her heart beat a little faster, too.

"It's best you come downstairs," she said, taking the hatbox and putting it away, high up in a closet. We were safe there, but it wasn't particularly cheerful.

Four Eyes in the Dead of Night

As we lay up there in the closet for several years, our legs got all stiff. Taxi Wollmar's oilcloth got even more cracked, because he was lying in such a strange position. We often heard Sophie and Baby Lotta (two dachshunds) barking outside the closet. They were probably hoping we would come down, so they could chew on us a little.

Early one morning, Christina left her husband (you remember, the one who called Little Bear "Filthy Bear"). And just think, the only things she took with her that morning were her toothbrush and the hatbox with us teddy bears in it.

We ended up in a little cottage in a park in Stockholm. It was cold and damp, but there was a working wood fireplace. You had to carry water in from the yard, and there was an outhouse out back.

We loved it, because we got to get out of the hatbox and sit on the deep window ledge with a view of the garden.

One dark night we heard strange noises under our window.

"It's probably robbers again," said Huggy Yellow. "Trying to dig their way in."

Christina and all of us were so scared. Christina called a friend (who, stupidly enough, lived more than a hundred miles away), in case we might need to be rescued.

He said to turn off all the lights and shine the flashlight out the window.

"Do I have to open the window?" asked Christina.

In the end, she dared to do it, and guess what she saw.

Four glowing eyes. Then she saw they belonged to two badgers who were busy building a nest under the house.

"How nice that there are badgers in the middle of the city!" said Christina.

After that, she didn't care about the digging noises under the floor. She's such a great friend of animals, Christina is. Though sometimes we wondered which was more dangerous for teddy bears — dachshunds or badgers.

When the dachshunds came to visit, Christina would say, "Are badgers dangerous for dachshunds, or is it the other way around?"

When they left, Christina told us, "Imagine how lonely I'd be here without you. How could I have kept you in that closet before?"

Meles meles (badger)

At the Toy Auction

ow I think I'll talk about the time Christina and I went to an auction house. That day they were selling only toys. In the catalogue we saw three teddy bears, a stuffed dog, ninety-four dolls, and a whole lot of other toys. Before the bidding, we visited a room in back of the auction hall to see the teddy bears and the dog. They each had a string around their middle. On the strings were labels with numbers on them.

"We're really worried about where we'll end up," said the big teddy (no. 1).

"Yes, because we'd love to go to the same place," said the little teddy bear, "now that we've become best friends and all ..."

"Not a chance," said no. 1. "It's mostly German antique dealers here. They don't care about teddy bears; they're just out to make a fast buck by selling us in the United States. The Americans will pay *anything* for an antique teddy bear."

"I'll probably go to someone nice," said the yellow teddy bear (no. 3). "I'm not all that antique, you know."

The dog just sighed.

Christina and I crossed our fingers for them. We went and sat down in the auction hall. I got to have my own chair. The place was full of serious buyers who thought Christina was crazy because she had a teddy bear with her.

A boy came in and put no. 1 up on a pedestal. The auction started.

"A Steiff, button missing, 1920s, new soles, do I hear sixteen hundred?" the auctioneer rattled away into the microphone. "Seventeen! Eighteen! Nineteen!" shouted the bidders all at the same time. Some just lifted a finger; that meant that they were offering another hundred crowns.

"Three thousand!!!" shouted a woman. The other bidders understood that there was no point in continuing. She had decided no. 1 was going to be hers.

The lady who bought him was an English collector. Luckily, she also bought no. 2, and the dog. But she didn't want no. 3; he wasn't antique enough.

"Imagine, teddy bears as *investment opportunities*," said Christina, sighing. "Well, it won't be like that with you!"

"That's good," I said (although I'm not sure what an "investment opportunity" is).

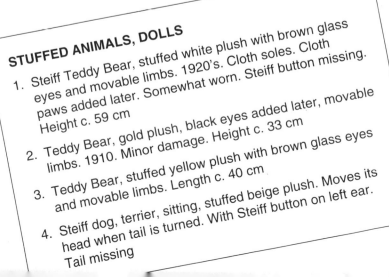

Now it was no. 3's turn to be sold

It's come to this because of the collectors. And maybe because of Mr. Bialosky, who wrote *The Teddy Bear Catalog*, where you can look up what different categories of teddy bears are worth. The older they are, the more they're worth. Mr. Bialosky warns against buying bears that have flat heads, are bald or blind, have loose arms or legs, torn soles, false stuffing (when the owner has replaced a hay or excelsior stuffing with something modern). All of that brings the price down. Forget about those kinds of teddy bears if you want to make a good buy. The best deal is a teddy bear in *mint condition*. That means the poor old bear has never even been used. Best of all, he should have lived his whole life in the original carton.

Some people think Christina is a teddy-bear collector. That's all wrong. She *has* certain teddy bears, and always has had them. Others came later. But she doesn't want to have as many as possible, and she doesn't care if they're a little beat up. Mr. Bialosky would probably faint if he saw Little Bear.

Hi, Mr. Bialosky!

Well, think about it, Mr. Bialosky. It's teddy bears with a soul you're putting a price tag on. Marking them down for baldness and blindness is *terribly* unsympathetic. You should start giving some soul to your poor unused teddy bears, still in their cartons, instead. Otherwise, you might as well collect model cars.

STUFFED ANIMALS, DOLLS

1. Steiff Teddy Bear, stuffed white plush with brown glass eyes and movable limbs. 1920's. Cloth soles. Cloth paws added later. Somewhat worn. Steiff button missing. Height c. 59 cm

2. Teddy Bear, gold plush, black eyes added later, movable limbs. 1910. Minor damage. Height c. 33 cm

3. Teddy Bear, stuffed yellow plush with brown glass eyes and movable limbs. Length c. 40 cm

4. Steiff dog, terrier, sitting, stuffed beige plush. Moves its head when tail is turned. With Steiff button on left ear. Tail missing

Now I'll End This Book, and Say Thank You

It felt good to tell the antique dealers off, as I did in the last chapter. Having done that, I think almost everything I'd planned to say has been said. Christina can take over the writing now, if there's anything more to add.

"Yes, I have a few more things to say," said Christina. "A little more about Winnie-the-Pooh, and about teddy bears in England, and an afterword. But it's hard for me to write that."

"We'll ask some human expert to write it for you," I said, "since I'm actually a *little* interested in what such people think about teddy bears …"

"What a great idea," said Christina. "And I'll get out of doing it. You ask."

"O.K.," I said. "But listen, can we teddy bears be really sure now?"

"Sure about what?" asked Christina.

"That we won't ever end up in the attic again," I said.

"Absolutely!" said Christina. "Can't you see that I've understood the teddy bear's importance for man? And especially *my* teddy bears' importance for *me*? You'll never get put in the hatbox again. Unless it's a question of making a movie about it, of course."

Oh yes, there's one thing I forgot to mention: these days we are with Christina all day long at her job. We've all become movie stars. We teddy bears, I mean. Here's how it happened:

Maria's teddy bear

One of Christina's best friends is named Maria. She's a cinematographer. When she was little, the same thing happened to her big yellow teddy bear that happened to Uncle Harry's Teddy Bear: he broke open and the sawdust started running out. Maria's mama put him in the broom closet, so he wouldn't make such a mess. Maria checked on him often, there in the closet. And then one day he was gone!

"I still miss him," says Maria.

Maria heard about Christina's teddy-bear book that never got written.

"What if we do a teddy-bear film, instead," she suggested.

"What a great idea!" said Christina.

And so the teddy-bear book got put off another couple of years. The best thing about that was that we teddy bears got to act in the film. Taxi Wollmar, too.

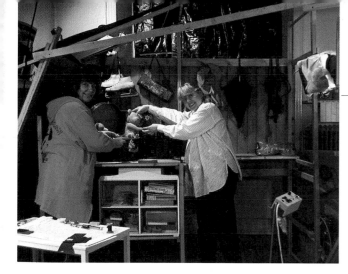

They trick-filmed us, so it looked as if we were moving and talking. Real human actors spoke for us. Christina and Maria had to learn to do *animation*. That means they would shoot one frame at a time. Then they would move a teddy bear about a quarter of an inch and shoot again. And move and shoot, move and shoot. When they put all the frames together and showed the film, it looked as if we teddy bears were moving by ourselves.

It's hard to do and takes forever. Even when we really get going, we can finish only half a minute of film a week.

"Well, it was just as you suspected," Maria told Christina when they looked at the film. "Your teddy bears are able to come to life, under certain circumstances!"

"They're always alive," said Christina. "But they don't move if we're looking."

And that's the truth.

Now I can't write any more. I have to rest up to get in shape. Acting is a demanding profession.

Oh, I almost forgot. Last summer, on Christina's birthday, her friend Gertie came by. She had the cutest sun bear with her. The bear was wearing a lace bonnet. She jumped right up and sat in my lap!

"Oh, look! There's my daddy," she explained to everybody at the party. "And that's my little brother," she added, pointing at Putte-Malajjo. "And my name is Baby Gertie, and this is all so much fun!"

She was right. And I thank you all!

Big Bear

Author, movie star, father of two

Thank You, Big Bear!

Thanks, Big Bear, for writing most of this book for me. Some things were easier for you to sniff out with your old teddy-bear nose, and a lot became clearer for me when I could see it with your teddy-bear eyes.

When you sit here on my desk in your little chair, and I look into your deep brown eyes, it brings me back. I can see the little girl I once was. And behind her is my father. You remind me a little of each other, you and my imaginative father. I can make out my mother, but she's not as clear. I learned later, when I grew up, that it was multiple sclerosis that made her ill so often.

The more you wrote, Big Bear, the more the memories came back: pictures I hadn't seen and thoughts I hadn't thought for years. Thanks, my dear Big Bear, for the memories. We've had fun, you and I!

Shepard's sketch of Piglet

Eeyore, Pooh, Kanga, Piglet, and Tigger, who today live at the New York Public Library

Thank You, Pooh!

Now I want to thank another teddy bear, Winnie-the-Pooh (and A. A. Milne, who wrote about him).

I've just reread both Pooh books, and they were still as good. Maybe I find other things in them than I saw when I was little. But I still think *Winnie-the-Pooh* and *The House at Pooh Corner* are masterworks of world literature.

Most people I know agree, though they add, "But when I was little I didn't get what they were all about."

First I thought there must be something wrong with them, but now I've heard the same thing from so many reliable people that I start thinking there must have been something wrong with me. It's very possible *Winnie-the-Pooh* is a book for adults.

Milne (1882–1956) was already a well-known author when he started writing poems in the magazine *Punch* about his son, Christopher Robin, and his toys. Light plays and novels, essays and light verse were his specialty otherwise.

A colleague at *Punch* suggested that Milne let the artist Ernest Howard Shepard illustrate the poems. Milne wasn't so sure, until he saw some sample drawings that Shepard did for him. At that point it became clear that Shepard would illustrate both the poems in *Punch* and the books that followed. (First came a collection of the poems.)

Shepard visited Cotchford Farm (in Hartfield, Sussex), where Milne lived, to make sketches of Christopher Robin, Pooh, Piglet, Eeyore, Tigger, and Kanga. Unfortunately, Baby Roo had been lost. Owl and Rabbit were Milne's inventions, so Shepard had to draw them using museum models.

It wasn't the real Pooh, however, that modeled for the book; Shepard thought his own son's teddy bear, Growler, had a better shape.

Winnie-the-Pooh came out in 1926 and became an instant success. Milne followed up with another book of poetry and another Pooh book, *The House at Pooh Corner*. That one came out in 1928 (when Christopher Robin was eight years old), making Milne world famous. Loads of fan mail arrived for Milne, Pooh, and Piglet, and for Christopher Robin (the *book's* Christopher Robin). The real Christopher Robin was forced to answer the letters.

After reading Christopher Milne's memoirs, I understand that it probably wasn't as wonderful being Christopher Robin as I had imagined when I was little. After reading *Winnie-the-Pooh,* you might think that Milne was the world's best dad, always telling stories (sort of like my father). Actually, Milne was only a master at writing about his little son; he had no idea how to play with him or tell him stories.

Milne sat in his study all the time, writing, while Christopher Robin was upstairs in the nursery with his nanny (his live-in babysitter). He saw his parents only for a little while after breakfast, a short visit after five o'clock tea, and a few minutes after dinner. Then Nanny would come and get him for his evening bath. And it was Nanny, not Milne, who read him a good-night story and gave him a hug, before she went to bed in the room next door to his. With few exceptions, Christopher Robin never heard a single chapter from *Winnie-the-Pooh* until his nanny read the book to him.

Nanny meant everything to Christopher Robin. You can imagine the shock he got, at nine years old, when he was sent away to boarding school. Without Nanny, and without Pooh.

And with that, the mystery of why Christopher Robin had to leave Pooh and all the others was solved. Maybe I had had a feeling that school had something to do with it, but I never would have guessed it would be something so cruel.

Nanny wasn't needed any longer at the Milnes', so she had to quit. That could have been one more tragedy, but it wasn't. At last, she could marry the man who had been waiting several years for her. Her married name was Olive Brockwell. Naturally, Christopher Milne dedicated his memoirs to her.

At boarding school, everyone had read about Christopher Robin and his toys. He was teased so much that he started to hate the book's Christopher Robin. From that time on, he called himself only Christopher Milne.

Eventually, he had a better relationship with his father. Cricket and literature were their common interests. On school holidays, Milne read for his family. One of their favorite books was *The Wind in the Willows.* Christopher Milne writes that the most moving chapter in the book was "The Piper at the Gates of Dawn." That's when his mother would

A. A. Milne, Christopher Robin, and Pooh, 1926

take out her handkerchief. His father liked the chapters about Mr. Toad better.

Today, Christopher Robin still gets letters from people who think he's always out skipping around in the woods with his old teddy bear. Even though he's a grownup man, close to retirement age. He and his wife run a bookshop in a small town. (I won't say which one, because he doesn't like people coming around to stare at him. I really have a hard time not going there myself.)

Where are Pooh and the others today? Roo, of course, is lost, but the rest are on display at the New York Public Library, at the Donnell Library Center on Fifty-third Street and Fifth Avenue. They were evacuated during World War II to America.

"Don't you miss Pooh and Piglet?" people always ask Milne.

"No," he answers. "I finished playing with those old things a long time ago."

England Is a Land of Teddy Bears

In England, teddy bears are appreciated by both children and grownups. Maybe Pooh broke the ice. Or was it the other way around: that such a book could have been written only in a country like England? I don't know. But a land of teddy bears it is.

Not that there are more teddy bears than in other places, but those that are there have such high status. Often they stay with their owners their whole lives. (Even if in the whole United Kingdom there are some neglected teddy bears.)

Teddy bears are well organized and quite naturally take part in social activities and teddy-bear festivities. Some examples are Bear Bank Holiday (in August), Teddy Bear Day (October 27, Teddy Roosevelt's birthday), and the teddy bear festival in Battersea Park, London (in August). The biggest and most important was the Teddy Bear Rally, arranged by the late Marquess of Bath in his castle garden. Tens of thousands of teddy bears (with their owners) went there to picnic. The marquess joined them with his own teddy bears.

Peter Bull and Theodore

Peter Bull with Delicatessen / Aloysius

Aloysius in Brideshead Revisited

Margaret Thatcher's teddy bear, Humphrey

The Marquess of Bath at a teddy-bear meeting

The chairman for the meeting was Archibald Chairbear. The "rally" was a fund-raiser, to collect money for sick children.

In England, no one so much as raises an eyebrow if a grownup goes to a teddy bears' picnic with his teddy bear.

Older gentlemen

Older gentlemen are especially fond of teddy bears. I had the pleasure of meeting one of them, the actor Peter Bull (who, among other roles, played the Russian ambassador in *Dr. Strangelove*). He lived in a small, elegant (but cold) flat on King's Road in London, with some hundred teddy bears. I asked if he'd had them since he was a boy.

"Oh no," said Peter Bull. "My *real* teddy bear ... that was a traumatic experience ... One day when I came home from school — I was probably about twelve then — Teddy wasn't sitting on my bed, as he usually was. I asked my mother where he was. 'Oh yes, your teddy,' said my mother, lightly. 'I gave him to the Red Cross's toy collection. You're much too old for Teddy now.'"

Peter Bull never got over that grief; I think he hated his mother for the rest of his life.

Once, after talking about it on television, he was flooded with teddy bears, sent in by sympathetic viewers.

"But nothing could ever replace my *real* teddy bear," said Peter Bull.

Still, little Theodore came to mean a lot to him as a companion on his travels all over the world. He always came along for TV appearances. And then there was Delicatessen! He was the big teddy bear who became world famous as Aloysius in the English television series *Brideshead Revisited*. Peter Bull insisted that the teddy bear, Aloysius (who had grown into his role so well that the name stayed with him), get a contract as an actor, not as a "rental prop." The contract gave him the right to have a stand-in for dangerous scenes, and home travel whenever the filming schedule allowed it. Aloysius is the only teddy bear who has left his paw print in the sidewalk in front of Grauman's Chinese Theater (now Mann's) in Hollywood. (Peter Bull didn't succeed, however, in getting him included in "Spotlight," the American professional actors' listing.)

As long as he lived, Peter Bull was the natural guest of honor at all teddy-bear festivities. He died in 1984.

There are many other famous teddy bears in England. Humphrey is one example. She (yes, it's a she) belongs to the former Prime Minister, Margaret Thatcher. Like her owner, she was a politician. She participated in several election campaigns and collected money for charity. But best of all, she liked staying home and taking it easy at 10 Downing Street.

Some English leaders of Parliament have a teddy-bear club. They meet now and then, with their teddy bears. One of them is said to have sixteen bears.

Royal Teddy Bears

The royal teddy bears are well known. The Queen Mother's is named Lady Elizabeth. Prince Charles has a big yellow one his mother gave him, named Teddy. He took Teddy with him to boarding school, a good example for British schoolboys. These days, Teddy lives in Kensington Palace. The young princes have gotten so many teddy bears from people all over the United Kingdom that most of them have had to be given to charity.

There's a teddy-bear organization called Good Bears of the World. It collects money to buy teddy bears for children who are in the hospital. British doctors claim that children recover more quickly if they have a teddy bear in bed with them who is being treated for the same problem.

The status of teddy bears can also be seen in British museums. In London alone, there are three museums with well-preserved teddy bears: Bethnal Green, Pollock's, and London Toy and Model Museum (right now closed for renovation). Of course, they have other toys as well, but they have a lot more teddy bears than other toy museums. In England, people respect and take care of their teddy bears, so they last a lifetime. And then they end up in museums. Or in retirement communities for old teddy bears.

That's how it is in England, the land of teddy bears.

Some ten thousand teddy bears at the Marquess of Bath's in May 1979

Afterword

by Johan Cullberg, Senior Physician and Associate Professor in Psychiatry

Dear Big Bear,

It is fun and flattering that you have asked me to write an afterword for this book. If I were a teddy bear, I would also wonder what those who are experts on the soul have to say about teddy bears.

Let me reassure you right now — we have only good things to say about you. It's even true that, without you, we humans would have a much harder time. To tell you the truth, it isn't only teddy bears, but also other stuffed animals and dolls. Even some rags which don't have the faintest resemblance to animals are interesting to researchers. That's because children love them so much. Researchers become curious, maybe even a little envious.

Your first loves are *not only* the people who take care of you. Of course, you like them very much. That's how it is with your parents in the beginning. What baby wouldn't love a mother who gave it milk when it was hungry, who felt nice and warm, who sang for it, who changed its diaper when it was wet, who washed it with a soft cloth and powdered it afterward?

But you teddy bears can't do any of that! And you don't need to, either, to be loved. You can do something else: you can allow us to be creative. And that's something really remarkable and fantastic. I'll try to explain it, as much as I understand it myself.

By the time we humans are about one year old, we've gotten everything we need from our parents (we hope so, anyway). We believe, and it's true in a way, that we are the center of the universe. If we cry, they come running; if we laugh, they laugh back.

But as a baby grows and begins to crawl, then to walk, everything starts getting more difficult. The things he has believed in, relied on, and demanded aren't working anymore. His parents don't come as quickly when he cries for them to be there. They're paying attention to each other, instead, or to others; maybe they even start leaving him with a babysitter. It's really quite a difficult time for the child, those first few years. It's not very often that things are what he had thought they would be.

Fortunately, there's a lot of wonder and fun, too. Just think of all the things to be discovered and learned. But that fantastic old feeling of being the center of the universe for a parent is more difficult to sustain as the child has to share his place with others. At this point, we are forced to develop a center *within ourselves*. Creating that center is something many of us won't succeed at if we don't get some good help when we're little.

This is where toy animals, among other things, help us along. You can do that just by being there, by letting us use our imagination. In the beginning, when we are really little, you're there for us as our make-believe and replacement mama. An actual teddy bear probably isn't needed yet — a soft rag, a piece of silky cloth, or a little pillow to hug, smell, and suck on is usually enough.

And God help the person who takes it away when the child is tired or upset. If he can no longer control people, at least the child can control his piece of cloth, which he has actually given a soul.

But what kind of soul is it the child has created with his pet blanket? Well, it's not a real mother, nor is it just a fantasy mother. The neat thing is that your rags and stuffed animals become a kind of bridge for the child, when he becomes his own person, accepting that his mother is one human being and he is another.

You allow the child to decide everything, to love you and hug you. But he can also bite, pull, and tear at you and you don't complain, and you don't go away. That makes it a little easier for the child to accept that his mother isn't meeting his every demand any longer.

So the child starts creating a world in his imagination that will help him through life. You are always there for him, no matter what happens, and that's why he loves you. Actively creating this world of his own is an important experience for the child. We can understand this when we see how much an adult's creativity and fantasy are like a child's. They come out in just that "transitional area" between reality and our inner world. To talk intimately with each other, to read and write, to paint, to make music, to dance — all this has something to do with play. We can train ourselves this way. Playing is actually a much more remarkable activity than most adults imagine it to be.

Later, when the child gets a little older, the time comes for a real doll and teddy-bear world. That's when you teddy bears become real for him, not just soft and cuddly things that can be treated any which way. As his teddy bears, you become his friends, not just replacements for the parents he can't own entirely. You share the child's life and help him be brave at the doctor's office, or sad at night when his parents or brothers and sisters have been mean. You can do anything the child wants you to, and that can be good for him, since it's hard for him to do everything he would like to do: fly, live out in the woods without being afraid, talk to animals, win out over someone much stronger, and other terribly difficult things.

Another thing that's good about teddy bears is that the child doesn't have to feel there is always someone else making the decisions. And because it's not all that terribly important whether you teddy bears are girls or boys (although, as a matter of fact, you usually are boys, right?), there never have to be any of those troublesome boy-girl problems that so often come up between human children.

You teddy bears are also not a bit interested in being important and powerful. If there's something we humans have trouble with, it's dealing with one another's sense of importance. But we become happier, better people when we're with someone who doesn't care about such things, because then we can relax.

Sooner or later, you're bound to wind up in the attic, or thrown away. Your life has ended then for that person, but he may still carry your memory with him. In my case, the end came when I decided to operate on my teddy bear. I was so terribly curious about how we looked inside that I cut a hole in my teddy bear's stomach. Inside, there was only excelsior. I was disappointed, but I started to understand that I would have to find out about things another way. And so I did. But thank you in any case for everything we shared.

Warmest regards,

Teddy-Bear Literature

A personal list of books that we like that were mentioned in Big Bear's Book *and used as source material. Books about bears (real bears) and toys in general are not included.*

ABOUT AND AROUND POOH

A. A. MILNE
When We Were Very Young. Poems about (among others) Christopher Robin and his toys. London: Methuen, 1924; New York: Dutton, 1924; Dutton, 1992.

Winnie-the-Pooh. London: Methuen, 1926; New York: Dutton, 1926; Dutton, 1991.

Now We Are Six. Second book of poems. London: Methuen, 1927; New York: Dutton, 1927; Dutton, 1992.

The House at Pooh Corner. London: Methuen, 1928; New York: Dutton, 1928; Dutton, 1991.

Winnie-the-Pooh has been translated into many languages. In Russian, he's called *Vinnie-Poch*; in Japanese, *Kuma no Pu-San*; in Latin, *Winnie Ille Pu*; in Esperanto, *Winnie-la-Pu*; and in Swedish, *Nalle Puh.*

ERNEST H. SHEPARD / BRIAN SIBLEY, editor
The Pooh Sketchbook. Shepard's Pooh sketches. London: Methuen, 1982; New York: Dutton, 1984.

CHRISTOPHER MILNE
The Enchanted Places. Christopher Milne's memoirs. London, Eyre Methuen, 1974; New York: Dutton, 1975.

The Path through the Trees. London: Methuen, 1979.

FREDERICK C. CREWS (pen name)
The Pooh Perplex. Parodies of scientific writings, analyzing Pooh. New York: NAL-Dutton, 1965.

Many people have written new books using Shepard's illustrations: *Pooh's Cookbook, Pooh's Party Book,* etc. They are like thin soup — boring.

CHILDREN'S BOOKS

KENNETH GRAHAME
The Wind in the Willows. New York: Scribner's, 1908; Trafalgar, 1992.

SELMA LAGERLÖF
The Wonderful Adventures of Nils. Garden City, N.Y.: Doubleday, 1968 (first published, 1907); Buccaneer, 1992.

JOHANNA SPYRI
Heidi. New York: Macmillan, 1962 (first published, 1884); NAL-Dutton, 1992.

NON-FICTION BOOKS

PEGGY & ALAN BIALOSKY
The Teddy Bear Catalog. New York: Workman Publishing, 1980.

PETER BULL
A Hug of Teddy Bears. New York: NAL-Dutton, 1984.

PAULINE COCKRILL
The Teddy Bear Encyclopedia. New York: Dorling Kindersley, 1993.

MARY HILLIER
Teddy Bears, a Celebration. London: Ebury Press, 1985; New York: Beaufort Books, 1985.

MARGARET HUTCHINGS
Teddy Bears and How to Make Them. New York: Dover Publications, 1964.

HELEN KAY
The First Teddy Bear. Owings Mills, Md.: Stemmer House, 1985.

RAMONA & DESMOND MORRIS
Men and Pandas. Why people like pandas (and teddy bears) so much. New York: McGraw-Hill, 1966.

PATRICIA N. SCHOONMAKER
A Collector's History of the Teddy Bear. Cumberland, Md.: Hobby House Press, 1981.

D. W. WINNICOT
Playing and Reality. New York: Routledge, Chapman and Hall, 1994.

Teddy-Bear Organization

There are probably more, but this is the one we know about.

GOOD BEARS OF THE WORLD
Donates teddy bears to children all over the world who've been through earthquakes, floods, and other disasters, as well as to homeless or abused children living in shelters. Police officers sometimes carry these bears in their cars.

Headquarters: P.O. Box 13097, Toledo, Ohio 43613
Tel/fax: 419-531-5365

Dues are $11 per year. Lifetime membership is $100. One dollar will get you a copy of the club magazine, *Bear Tracks.*

Teddy-Bear Museums

Here are some toy museums with nice teddy bears. (The toy museum in Paris is no fun at all.)

UNITED STATES

The Carrousel Shop and Museum
505 W. Broad Street
Chesaning, Michigan 48616
517-845-7881

This has over four hundred teddy bears, mostly antiques. Many of the bears come with stories about how they happened to be included in the Michaud collection. There are also full-size replicas and miniatures.

Children's Museum of Indianapolis
P.O. Box 3000
Indianapolis, Indiana 46206
317-924-5431

This has about a hundred bears, ranging from a 1908 white Steiff to modern artists' originals. Their bears also have family histories and at Christmas there is a bear-oriented holiday display with animated bears.

Theodore Roosevelt Birthplace
28 E. Twentieth Street
New York, New York 10003
212-260-1616

This has a replica of a Steiff bear, along with other memorabilia related to the bear craze of the 1920s — books, photos, and original Clifford Berryman cartoons.

Margaret Woodbury Strong Museum
1 Manhattan Square
Rochester, New York 14607
716-263-2700

This has fewer than ten bears, but two are original Steiffs and two are antique stuffed pull-toy bears. The museum's annual Teddy Bear Fair, which is attended by dealers from all over the country, features a teddy bear hospital and usually a Steiff relative (one year, a granddaughter) to sign Steiff bears.

Teddy Bear Castle Museum
431 Broad Street
Nevada City, California 95959
916-265-5804

The museum, which is located in an 1860 cottage, has well over seven hundred bears of all sizes, the oldest being a bear on wheels from around 1880. Nevada City hosts the Annual International Teddy Bear Convention, featuring picnics, circus acts, and bear contests.

Teddy Bear Museum of Naples
2511 Pine Ridge Road
Naples, Florida 33942
813-598-2711

This has nearly three thousand teddy bears from all over the world, including antiques and one-of-a-kind artist's originals. The bears range in size from five-eighths of an inch to eight feet tall. The museum also has a teddy-bear hospital (all insurance accepted), bear-making classes, and a "libeary" with reference and story books.

SWEDEN

Tidö Castle Toy Museum
Västerås
Tel: (021) 530 17 or 530 42

Among the 40,000 toys are a few teddy bears. (The King of Sweden's is there, and the last Russian czar's.)

ENGLAND

Bethnal Green Museum of Childhood
Cambridge Heath Road, London
Tel: (081) 980 2415

Well worth the subway ride to Bethnal Green Station. Lots of fine teddy bears with childhood photographs.

Cotswold Teddy Bear Museum
76 High Street
Broadway, Cotswolds, Worcs. WR12 7AJ
Tel: (0386) 858 323

Over 800 teddy bears. Many famous, e.g., A. A. Milne's (not Christopher Robin's Winnie the Pooh — he is in New York — but Milne's own teddy bear).

London Toy and Model Museum
23 Craven Hill, London
Tel: (071) 262 7905 or 262 9450

Museum with good collections, lots of teddy bears, and a well-stocked gift shop. Right now closed for renovation (June 1994).

Pollock's Toy Museum
1 Scala Street, London
Tel: (071) 636 3452

Old private toy museum on several rickety floors. The teddy bears are old and worn and with lots of character. Fun toys to buy on the ground floor.

The Teddy Bear Museum
19 Greenhill Street
Stratford-upon-Avon
Tel: (0789) 293 160

Hundreds of teddy bears from around the world, some very old. A teddy bears' library and a teddy bears' picnic.

Longleat House (Bath)
Tel: (0985) 844 400

Built 1580, and still owned and lived in by the same family. In 1966 the late Marquess of Bath established a drive-through wild animal reserve. Also museums, doll houses, teddy bears.

GERMANY

Museum der Firma Margarete Steiff
P.O. Box 1560
7928 Giengen an der Brenz
Tel: (7322) 13 13 98 or 13 13 11

The factory's own teddy bears (original and copies) from 1903 on.

Spielzeugmuseum
1 Karlstrasse 13
Nürnberg
Tel: (911) 231 31 64

Nice big toy museum with very few teddy bears. Nürnberg is the toy capital of Europe.

DENMARK

Legetøjsmuseet
Valkendorfsgade 13
Copenhagen
Tel: (33) 14 10 09

With the lovable teddy bears above, one in a scout uniform.

November 14, 1978, Sweden issued a stamp honoring teddy bears. The picture is from an old photograph. The stamp is no longer for sale.

Picture Credits

PHOTOGRAPHS

Nisse Peterson: Jacket, front & back, pages 8, 14–15
26–27 (books), 29 (rug), 30, 32, 60, 74–75
Maria Brännström: 31, 39, 44
Svante Sjöstedt: 11, 16, 17, 18, 19, 50
Steiff GmbH: 55, 56 (Steiff teddy bear), 59
Mark Michtom, Ideal Toys: 56 (Morris teddy bear,
Mark Michtom)
Bethnal Green Museum: 58 (girl)
Victoria and Albert Museum: 66 (sketch of Piglet)
National Portrait Gallery: 67
E. P. Dutton, Publisher: 66 (Pooh and friends today)
Nordic Museum (Stockholm): 58 (boy)
Bo Sundin: 65
Per Thunarf: 41
Patrick Ward/IBL: 68
Pressens Bild: 70–71
Swedish Radio Picture Archive: 56 (Theodore Roose-
velt)
Klas Andersson: 38
The other photographs are from family albums, or
taken by Christina Björk

ILLUSTRATIONS

Inga-Karin Eriksson: initial letters, vignettes
Ernest Howard Shepard/Lennart Sane Agency: 17,
46–49, 66 (Piglet), 67
Lena Anderson: 22–25, 27, 28
Fibben Hald: 42–43
Samaritaine's catalogue (1909): 58
Ville de St Denis' catalogue (1903): 54
Åhlén & Holms' catalogue (1911): 59
Clifford Berryman: 57 (top two)
Seymour Eaton: 57 (bottom)